Thanks To...

My youngest son who begged me to think of one more story every night.

My youngest daughter who loved this story that I made up and my silly drawings of the dragon.

Our children who have blessed their Daddy and I with wonderful grandchildren whom have giggled at my telling the story to them and invited me to read it to their class at school.

The friends and family who proofed this several times and encouraged me to get it printed.

Note to the reader:

The Dragging Dragon can be an interactive story.
The dragon is not named and a name can be provided
by one or several listeners.
My children and grandchildren love to pick a different name
at every blank line with an *asterisk.
When they pause or stutter a name
"Ah," "Um" or "I Don't Know," becomes the name
until the next *asterisk.
(This is usually accompanied by lots of giggles.)

When reading to a large group
I make copies of the words "YAY," and "BOO," as well as
the pictures of the dragons and flowers.
The audience may then hold the copies up
at the storyline of their picture.
Enjoy the fun.   Gayle Gorrell

The Dragging Dragon
By Gayle Gorrell

I have a story of a dragon but I can't remember its' name.
Perhaps you could help me, Pleeeeease?
When you see a blank line with an asterisk
like this, *_____,
call out a name you like.
You can keep saying that name at every blank or change it
when an *asterisk appears again.

This dragon is so slow and sad
It just drags its sluggish body around to hunt for food.
It just eats fallen leaves and grass,
not even bothering to reach up to find fresh leaves.

When the story is sad you can say "BOO" if you want,
and when the story sounds happy you can say "YAY".

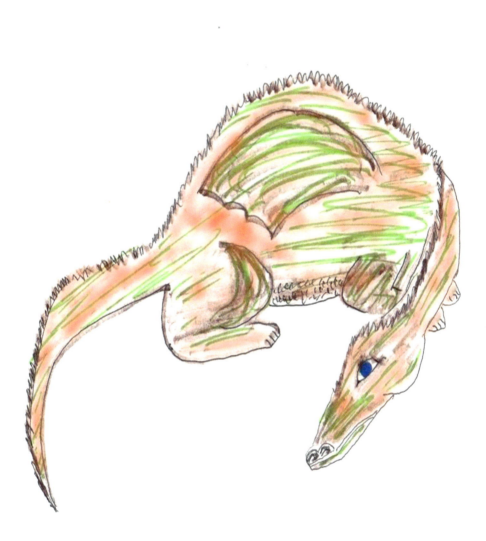

Once upon a time there was a sad, dull, less than ordinary dragon named *_____.
The reason _____ was sad, and never smiled, breathed fire or roared was because _____ had heard stories of some famous dragons that had wonderful powers.
You see, the dragon named *_____, was not scary, could not be invisible, could not fly. _____ couldn't even sing or recite poetry and had no magic powers.
Why, this dragon was so boring and sad _____ couldn't even scourge the countryside or help out fair damsels in distress like it thought dragons were supposed to do.

BOO!

One day the dragon named *_____ noticed
A person walking by with a basket of flowers.
The person looked over at the pitifully sad _____
and asked, "Why have I never noticed you here before?"
Of course, this just made _____feel worse.
So the dragon named *_____ rolled over
and thought; "No one notices me, not even children passing by.
I am boring, plain, not even scary, can't breathe fire, can't be
invisible, can't fly, can't sing, can't quote poetry or do magic.
Then_____ moved away
to find more leaves and grass and cry."

BOO!

The person noticed, carefully walked closer to_____
and then said,
"Well, that is part of your problem; you eat boring food.
You need a change of pace.
"Here now, try some flowers.
I have a basket full of yellow ones you may eat," she said.
"Yummy, they smell so good. Thank you, thank you,"
thought the dragon named*_____ as it ate the flowers.
Just being noticed made _____ smile and it went to
find more yellow flowers, so happy knowing its diet wouldn't be
boring again.

YAY

Night came and _____ fell asleep.

The next day some children passing by yelled, "Look at the dragon, it is yellow!"

YAY!

The dragon named *_____ looked down and saw that it was true. Instead of boring brown, _____ was yellow!
"More flowers, I must eat more yellow flowers," said _____, while smiling from ear to ear.

YAY!

Of course, the dragon named *_____ still didn't do anything else special and after a while even a yellow dragon is no treat to see. So _____ began to be sad once more because no one paid attention to _____ or the yellow scales on its body.

BOO!

Finally, the dragon named *_____ remembered the friendly advice from the person with the delicious yellow flowers. _____ thought, "There needs to be a change. Ah yes! Maybe red flowers this time."

So _____ hurried off to find red flowers.

Sure enough, the next day the dragon named*_____
awoke to children screaming about a red dragon!
_____ was so happy to look and see its'
beautiful red scales that _____ walked over to make
friends with the children and their parents.
YAY!

Time passes as it always does and a red dragon that does nothing but come close to people, was no big deal again.
However, the dragon named *_____
had another idea. _____ had noticed a flower garden with lots of different colored flowers in it.
So _____ wondered what might happen if it ate a whole garden.
Would the dragon named *_____ get a tummy ache, a thorn in its throat, an allergy or itching?
Could there be dreaded stinky marigold breath?

BOO!

_____ ate the garden anyway then drifted off to sleep.

What do you think happened to _____?

The next morning the dragon named*_____ woke up to sounds of shouts and laughter. People were taking pictures and camera clicks were coming from all directions. _____ looked down and gasped. Smiling from ear to ear again, _____ watched as a bus load of visitors came to see the fantastic change.

YAY!

The dragon named *_____ was covered in polka dots and every day the dots were different color patterns.
Seeing the change in _____'s scales could never be boring and every smile from new visitors helped keep a smile on the dragon's face.
So _____ enjoyed a delicious colorful flower salad every day and lived happily ever after.

YAY!

Oh, by the way,
do you have a colorful flower garden?
Just *maybe* a polka dot dragon could show up
In your yard.

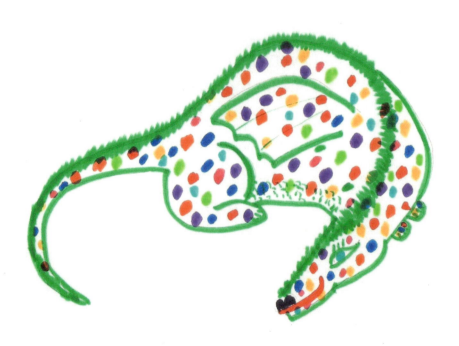

About the Author:
Gayle Gorrell
is a stay at home Momma with a wonderful Husband,
6 beloved Children,
fantastic Sons and Daughter in-laws,
several angelic Grandchildren,
and several perfect Great Grandchildren.
She likes volunteering and serving where she can.
As a longtime member of
The Church of Jesus Christ of Latter Day Saints
She Loves Heavenly Father, Jesus Christ and the influence The Holy Spirit has in her life.

Made in the USA
Columbia, SC
06 September 2024